Alfred a

67 day challenge

Written and illustrated by Stafford Dungey

www.alfredthemusician.com

Chapter 1 - The Time Bandit Guitar

It was the first day back to school in the sleepy village of Hightown, the year was 1995. Alfred's mum handed him his guitar and schoolbag then waved him goodbye as he made his way to the school entrance.

Alfred was 16 years old and like most teenagers, music was one of the few things that made him feel happy inside. Ever since he found his dad's collection of classic rock albums he had been obsessed with music and determined that one day he would play in a rock band.

Today was Wednesday, the best day of the week for Alfred as this meant music lessons with Mr. Harmonic which were a world away from the cold hard drudgery of double mathematics which took up most of the morning's tutorials.

Alfred sat next to his good friend Eddie, a guitar whizz kid. Eddie was always tinkering with electronics and guitars. His latest project was the construction of a groundbreaking new guitar sampler which allowed the guitar player to program the year of choice in via the control panel and the instrument would faithfully reproduce the sound of that era. Eddie's pride and joy was called the Time Bandit!

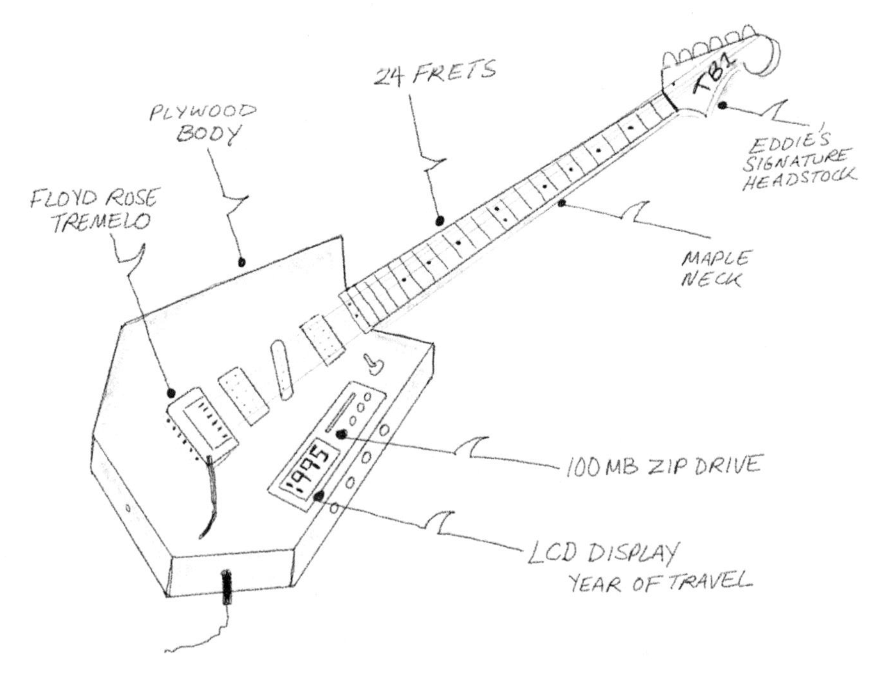

Mr. Harmonic began the lesson by announcing that he would be performing with his Rhythm and Blues band at the annual Summer Festival (as he had done every year since 1982). This was the one weekend of the year that Hightown would come alive! The town would burst into life, buzzing with artists, street performers, musicians and be crammed full of weird and wonderful events. A blast of positive energy would sweep through the town, even

Graham and Maureen from number 52 who would often turn their noses up at any talk of the event were seen letting their hair down (or what was left of it), apparently swaying to a soft jazzy number by The Enormous Small Band.

Alfred and Eddie shot their arms high in the air when Mr. Harmonic asked the class to name how many notes there were in the Chromatic Scale.
"Twelve!" exclaimed the pair in unison.

Alfred would often not remember the correct way to conjugate his French verbs or recall how to use BODMAS to find the answer to a decimal multiplication sum, but he knew all his scales and arpeggios and all the lyrics to the latest album by rock group 'Mr Scary.'

As soon as he would get home from school, Alfred would rush to his bedroom to work out how to play another one of their songs. Mr Scary were his all time favourite group. Their music was loud, fast and they were well known for their 'sick' riffs, played by virtuoso guitarist Kevin Slaughter. Their live shows included fireworks, pyrotechnics and even a large water canon which would spray the audience with cold H_2O, much to the delight of the hot and sweaty crowd. You can imagine the sheer joy that evening as Alfred was tucking into his tea, when he heard Alan Van Dyke on the radio announce that this year Mr Scary were to headline the Hightown Festival. Alfred nearly choked on his Pirate Pie as he attempted to digest this information.

Then Mr. Van Dyke revealed that there was to be a battle of the bands competition and the winner would get to perform live on the main stage at the festival and get to meet Mr Scary backstage at the event! Alfred's mum had to check for signs of life at this point, as her son had momentarily been struck dumb and was speechless for the first time in his life. His face was as pale as the greek yoghurt that was now placed before him awaiting to be consumed.

Overwhelming glee had given way to a rising wave of panic as Alfred realised that he had just 67 days to form a band and fulfil his dreams of rocking out on stage at the Hightown Summer Festival.

"The journey of a thousand miles begins with a single step" is a quote by motivational speaker Tony Robbins.

Chapter 2 - The Mission

After a restless nights sleep, Alfred awoke at 5am and contemplated the task that lay ahead of him. The prospect of getting a band together capable of winning a slot at the greatest show in Hightown filled him with equal amounts of fear and excitement. He set about immediately by writing a plan of action;

ALFRED'S 67 DAY CHALLENGE

- Ask Eddie to be in the band and find a drummer
- Practice every single day
- Book rehearsal room in the music department
- Enter the battle of the bands competition
- Win the competition and get Kevin Slaughter's autograph!

Alfred had now set out his intentions and there wasn't a moment to lose. He decided that he would read his plan aloud every morning when he woke up and every night before he went to sleep, in order to build his confidence and make himself unstoppable!

Later that day, Alfred found Eddie in the Music Department playing 'Stairway to Heaven' on a ukulele. As he played, Alfred told Eddie his plan. Eddie was also a huge Mr Scary fan and was on board and fired up for the challenge.

As the pair were about to make their way to History class, they could hear the haunting sound of Beethoven's 'Moonlight Sonata' emanating from the room below. The sound was captivating and the pair listened intently as they made their way down the stairs to get a glimpse through the porthole window. The beautiful sound of the piano was being played by Amy Loveknot who was warming up for her Grade 6 exam.

"Eddie..." whispered Alfred in a low voice,

"Can you make the Time Bandit sound like Beethoven?"

"Well..." replied Eddie, "technically it's possible but so far I've only managed to program samples back to the 1950s. It would take 6 months at least."

"Hmmm I wonder," thought Alfred "we've only got 67 days."

Miss. Loveknot with her large spectacles and long brown hair had already spotted the pair muttering outside before bellowing

"What do you want?"

Alfred could almost feel his brain exploding as he attempted to pull himself together and force the words out of his mouth to ask if she would like to be in his band.

"No!" She exclaimed, "I have too many exams, besides I'm already playing with Artichoke Wind!"

Then, out of nowhere appeared the pale handsome figure of Neil Artichoke, a year 12 prefect and Grade 8 music student as well as Musical Director for the school wind band.

"What are you two doing out of lessons?" he barked, "Leave at once, Amy must not be distracted!"

Without a second glance, the door was slammed shut and Alfred and Eddie were left to make their way to the History Department.

"We don't stand a chance of winning the competition if Artichoke Wind are playing," remarked Eddie.

"It's true," said Alfred "Neil Artichoke does win everything but... he doesn't have the Time Bandit guitar does he Eddie?"

Alfred paused for a moment, "We need that machine to sound like a rock and roll symphony if we are going to impress those judges... you work on programming Beethoven Eddie, I'll find us a drummer!"

The next morning, Alfred put up an advert on the Music Department notice board, it read:

As he pinned the notice to the board, he could hear the sound of drums coming from the rehearsal room.

He peered through the window to see Colin Bartlett practising on a three piece drum kit. His big round face always beaming with pride caught sight of Alfred.
"How can I help?" Colin said with a wide smile.
"I'm after a drummer to join our band and play in the battle of the bands competition." explained Alfred.
"I'd love to mate but I'm already playing with Artichoke Wind," he replied.
"Oh…ok never mind." said Alfred barely concealing his disappointment. He was beginning to wonder if there were any musicians left in the school who weren't already playing in Neil Artichoke's band! He left Colin to practice his paradiddles in peace.

Chapter 3 - The Audition

A whole week passed with still no prospect of finding a drummer, when one evening Alfred got a call from a boy named Tommy Knuckles. They arranged to meet the following day in the lunch break for an audition. Mr. Harmonic unlocked the rehearsal room and Alfred and Eddie tuned up their guitars and waited for the audition to begin.

A curly haired boy with red cheeks and a long ill fitting jumper appeared and took his seat at the drum stool. Alfred began proceedings.

"You must be Tommy."

"Please call me Knuckles." replied the boy.

"Why do they call you knuckles?" Alfred enquired.

Then, without warning as if this initiation had been well rehearsed several times before, the boy began making cracking noises in his neck, jaw and fingers leaving Alfred and Eddie feeling equal amounts of awe and horror.

"What the hell is that?" exclaimed Knuckles pointing at Eddie's guitar.

"This is a prototype guitar time sampler," replied Eddie with pride.

"You dial in the year via the control panel then flick the selector switch to activate the year."

"It looks really weird." said Knuckles.
"It's a work in progress...but listen to this!"
Eddie casually dialed in 1974 on the control panel and flicked the selector switch to rock mode. All of a sudden, the room was filled with the blistering guitar sound of Brian May as Eddie played the guitar solo to 'Killer Queen.' Then Eddie knocked the dial back to 1967 and the eye watering sound of Jimi Hendrix came blasting out of the speaker.
"What about Clapton?" asked Knuckles, now looking on in astonishment.
"Coming right up," replied Eddie as he cooly dialled in 1970 and launched into the opening riff of 'Layla' by Derek and the Dominoes. Eddie then dialled in 1963 and flicked the selector switch to Jazz mode and began to play the opening music to 'The Pink Panther', making his Time Bandit guitar honk like a saxophone.
"Wow!" exclaimed Knuckles, "Awesome! I mean, it looks horrible, but it sounds rad. Have you got a name for it?"
"It's called the Time Bandit MK1, or the TB1 for short."
"That's it!" Alfred exclaimed "The Time Bandits... that's the name of the band! What do you think?"
"I like it" agreed Eddie nodding his head.

"Sweet," replied Knuckles.

The lunch hour passed in the blink of an eye as the trio made their way through songs such as 'Hey Joe' by Jimi Hendrix, 'Paint it black' by the Rolling Stones and 'Smoke on the water,' by Deep Purple. Alfred and Eddie exchanged nods of approval on Knuckles' audition performance before offering him the permanent position of drummer in the band.

"RAD!" said Knuckles and began making cracking noises in his neck as they all made their separate ways to the afternoon lessons.

Within two weeks, Alfred now had a band and for the first time in his short life he felt like he had a purpose and was at the beginning of an adventure.

"Progress equals happiness" is a quote by motivational speaker Tony Robbins.

Chapter 4 - The Russian Classic

For the next fortnight, the trio spent every other lunch break rehearsing in the Music Department. They played through dozens of ideas whilst trying to find a song that was capable of winning the competition.
At home one evening after school, Alfred was doing his homework whilst listening to Alan Van Dyke play another Mr Scary song on his Drive Time show when Alfred's dad asked him how the band was going?
"We sound good dad, but I'm not sure it's what the judges are looking for," said Alfred as he mopped up the remaining gravy with his last roast potato.
"Don't try too hard to sound like everyone else," replied his dad. "Be yourself!"
Alfred's mum switched over Mr Van Dyke to BBC Radio 4 to listen to her favourite programme 'Just a Minute.'
"Turn it up!" requested Alfred's dad.
A presenter was speaking in a loud theatrical tone in a witty pompous style,
"Bumblebees would not be expected to sustain flight as they would need to generate too much power given their very very tiny wings," babbled the man.
A loud buzzer went off and the studio audience (joined by Alfred's mum and dad) fell into hysterical

laughter. At first, Alfred tried to work out why this was funny, but was all of a sudden hit by a Eureka moment!

"That's it!" cried Alfred, knocking the pepper pot onto the floor. "Flight of the Bumblebee!"
He ran upstairs leaving his dad with one ear against the radio, listening intently to the programme whilst his mum did the washing up.

Alfred immediately called Eddie on the landline who was in the middle of eating a bowl of chips and watching Star Trek.

"Eddie... listen! You need to program the Time Bandit to the year 1900!" exclaimed Alfred.

"Why?" replied Eddie chewing on another crinkle cut chip.

"We need to play 'Flight of the Bumblebee' it's a classical masterpiece." Alfred continued.

"I know." Eddie responded

"It's also ridiculously hard to play...it's one thing to make a guitar sound like a Russian composer but it's another thing altogether to play something so complicated at our first gig!"

"I know you can do it Eddie...just imagine the look on the Judges faces! " continued Alfred desperately trying to get Eddie to come round to the idea. There was a pause in the conversation as Eddie chewed the idea over in his head for a while.

"...Ok, let's try it!" Eddie sighed.

"Brilliant!" cheered Alfred punching the air in defiance.

The next day, Alfred went down to the Lord Louis Library and asked at reception if they had the 'Flight of the Bumblebee' on CD. The Librarian pointed to the Classical section on the CD display counter and Alfred rummaged through dozens of CDs until he happened upon a disk called 'Russian Classics.'

"Bingo!" thought Alfred.

Sure enough it was the opening track by Nikolai Rimsky-Korsakov. Alfred used his mum's library card and took the CD home and subsequently spent the whole weekend listening to it.

Meanwhile, Eddie barely saw daylight as he frantically uploaded samples to the Time Bandit's zip drive and made alterations to the circuit board with a soldering iron in one hand and a Mars Bar in the other!

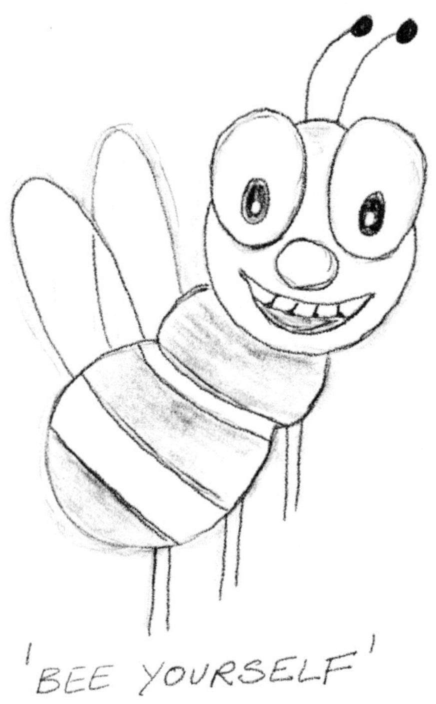

Chapter 5 - Six weeks to go

Every morning when he woke up, Alfred would try to visualise performing with his band and winning the competition. Then he would imagine playing at the Hightown Festival before actually getting to see Mr. Scary perform to a huge crowd, whilst getting soaked by the enormous on stage water canon. Some days he would be so deep in thought that his mum grew weary of his lack of response to her questions that she started to become concerned that her son was going deaf.

"DON'T FORGET YOUR SANDWICHES!" Alfred's mum shouted.

"Thanks Mum, BYE!" replied Alfred as he leapt out of his mum's Renault 4 and ran up to the School entrance.

He met up with Eddie and the pair made their way to assembly where the Headmaster Mr. Crouch announced that today there was to be a special performance by an exciting group of musicians.

"We are going to see a performance by Artichoke Wind," announced the headmaster as a large group of students made their way to the stage.

"Not again" whispered Eddie "This is the fifth time they've played in assembly this year!"

The band picked up their instruments and launched into 'Summer Loving,' from the hit musical Grease. Neil Artichoke moved around the stage like a bullfighter with tight blue jeans and greased back hair and gave a flawless performance, much to the delight of the girls on the front row who were transfixed by the prefect.

The song ended to rapturous applause from the teachers and Mr. Crouch walked back on stage to thank Neil and Artichoke Wind for such a delightful performance.

"I think I'm going to be sick," muttered Eddie.

"Well I guess it's not our cup of tea." Alfred whispered in reply, sitting low in his seat at the back of the auditorium.

Later that day, during their lunch break the trio met for their next rehearsal and began to practice the new Russian classic.

"Knuckles, don't start it too fast!" begged Eddie "Otherwise the Time Bandit will overheat!"

"Roger that," nodded Knuckles "I'll keep it at 125 beats per minute."

Knuckles would start the song on the hi hat cymbals before Eddie would descend down the A minor chromatic scale, then Alfred would come in with a

12 bar blues riff on the guitar as the song changed direction into a rock 'n' roll crossover before finally coming to a dramatic conclusion with Knuckles launching into a kamikaze drum roll on the cymbals.
"Flight of the rockin' Bumblebee!" came a voice that appeared from nowhere. Mr. Harmonic who could hear the trio practising from his office came in and was clearly impressed.
"That sounds excellent lads, would you like to play in next week's assembly?"
"Yes Sir!" Alfred, Eddie and Knuckles nodded enthusiastically.
"Great! Have you got a band name?" asked their teacher.
"Yes," answered Alfred, "We're the Time Bandits."
"Ok Time Bandits, I shall book you for next week's assembly…Don't be late!" added Mr. Harmonic as he left the room.

Alfred could hardly contain his glee later that evening as he told his mum and dad that his band would get to play their first ever performance.
"Can I come?" asked Alfred's mum.
"No! It's the school assembly mum." sighed Alfred, "You can come and watch us at the competition."
Alfred realised that there was only 6 weeks to go until

the festival. Every morning and before bed, he made sure that he read aloud his plan of action and would often visualise his band performing at The Battle of the Bands competition and playing live on the Main Stage at the Hightown Summer Festival.

Chapter 6 - the Assembly

It was the day of the assembly and Alfred was filled with nervous excitement as he was about to get his first taste of playing on stage in front of the whole school.

"Break a leg!" said his mum as the Renault 4 coughed and spluttered its way to the school drop off point.

Alfred ran into the Music Department with his guitar slung over his back to find that Knuckles and Eddie were already there. Mr. Harmonic told them to set up their gear and wait backstage until he called them out. Knuckles started setting up his drum kit whilst Eddie and Alfred began tuning up their guitars. The band sound checked the volume and made sure everything was working before heading into the corridor and waiting at the back of the Theatre. The seats began to fill up as students started to pour into the Auditorium. Knuckles was making anxious cracking noises in his neck and shoulders whilst Eddie was doing breathing exercises through his nostrils. Butterflies in the stomach were now making the trio feel sick as they waited patiently for Mr. Harmonic to appear.

"Ready guys?" said a voice from out of the darkness.

"Yes," replied the trio sheepishly.

"I'll go and introduce you, then you come on and play."
Mr. Harmonic disappeared behind the curtain and made his way to the front of the stage.
"Good morning. Today we have an exciting new band to play for you. They are going to perform 'The flight of the rockin' Bumblebee!' Please welcome, The Time Bandits!"
Alfred, Eddie and Knuckles gingerly made their way out onto the stage and into the dazzling glare of the stage lighting. They picked up their instruments and Knuckles counted them in perfectly whilst Eddie began his descent down the fretboard. They executed the song without a single mistake and in just over three and a half minutes it was all over. Before they knew it, the trio were basking in the glow of rapturous applause.
Alfred could feel his heart pumping in his chest as they made their way off the stage and into the dark corridor. The trio punched the air with happiness and relief.
"That was awesome!" exclaimed Knuckles with sweat dripping off his forehead.
"Well done lads!" interrupted Mr. Harmonic, as his head popped out from behind the curtain.
"That guitar sound is truly amazing!"

The trio made their way up the long corridor and into the Music Department where they were met at the top of the stairs by none other than Neil Artichoke accompanied by two girls, one either side of him.
"Interesting performance guys." Neil remarked.
"Of course, the tempo was a little andantino and you really shouldn't swing your quavers in a Russian classic."
Knuckles, who was visibly aggravated by this remark quickly responded,
"I'll kick you in the quavers Artichoke if you don't get out of the way."
"May I remind you that I am a prefect and I can report you for inappropriate behaviour… now move over and make way for the ladies."
Neil walked past with an air of authority as the two girls both giggling hysterically made their way down the stairs and out of sight leaving `Knuckles biting his tongue and clenching his fists.
"Don't let him wind you up." Alfred sympathised, as he could see his friend was fuming with rage.
"You really shouldn't swing your quavers," Eddie imitated the prefect in a mimicking voice,
"What a dork!"
"Leave it," sighed Alfred "We've just played our first gig and the audience loved it, we should be proud.

Next stop... Battle of the bands!" Alfred enthused. Alfred spent the next week feeling like he was floating on air as people he didn't even know came up to him and commented on the assembly performance asking him about the band and what music he was listening to. It was as if all of a sudden he was no longer invisible at school. Alfred knew one thing for sure, the feeling playing in a rock and roll band was electric and he wanted to do it again.

The weekend had arrived and Alfred and Eddie made their way to The Apollo Theatre at the top of the town. The lady at the reception gave them a form to fill in and a list of criteria required for entry into the prestigious Battle of the Bands competition.
It read as follows;

Battle of the Bands - Rules & Regulations
Apollo Theatre - Sat 15th May 1995

1) *Bands must submit a CD to the Apollo Theatre by Friday 9th May.*
2) *Each band's set must fill approximately 15 minutes but must not exceed 20 minutes.*
3) *Any damage caused or distasteful behaviour will result in automatic disqualification.*

2) *The Apollo Theatre will not be held accountable for any broken equipment, injuries or any other occurrences out of the staff's control.*
3) *All entrants must be able to guarantee that they will be able to perform at the Hightown Summer Festival on the 25th June in its entirety with the same person/s and instruments that competed at the aforementioned Battle Of the Bands event.*

Judging Criteria

- *Planning - evidence of performance planning.*
- *Originality - how unique did the songs sound?*
- *Material - did the band sound original?*
- *Appearance - did the band stand out?*
- *Stage presence - did the band use the stage effectively?*
- *Improvisation - did the band demonstrate improvisational skills?*
- *Entertainment Factor - did the band entertain?*

"Jumping butterballs Eddie!" exclaimed Alfred. "We need a CD to enter the competition!"

Eddie scratched his head before saying,
"We could try recording at the Hightown Studios."
"Amazing idea Eddie!" Alfred answered.
"Let's go over there now and see if we can book a recording session."

The pair made their way to the other side of town to Hightown Studios which was located in a basement underneath a Fish and Chip shop. They pressed the door buzzer and waited until a man with a shiny bald head and a friendly smile appeared.
"We'd like to book a recording session as soon as possible," requested Alfred.
"Come in," replied the softly spoken man.
"My name is Frank, I'm the producer. I'll show you around the studio."
He ushered Alfred and Eddie into the dimly lit rehearsal room where a band were getting ready to record a track.
"Let me show you the cockpit," offered Frank.
A narrow door that was heavily soundproofed went through into a control room where a myriad of gadgets and switches flickered and flashed around a computer screen in the centre that displayed meter readings and data.
"WOW!" exclaimed Alfred and Eddie in unison.

"You are looking at a Boeing flight console," explained Frank with pride.
"I'm a pilot during the week and I record bands at weekends. This console I managed to buy from a decommissioned 737 jet and I modified it to record audio."
Eddie was speechless and looked as if his jaw was about to hit the floor. Frank continued,
"It's fitted with a black box recorder with simulator effects including Vulcan bass, Concorde delays and Stealth compression." Frank the producer paused before adding, "Basically we can make even the most terrible band sound amazing!"
"Great!" said Alfred nervously "When can you book us in?"
"How about next Saturday?" replied Frank looking at his diary.
"Perfect " Alfred agreed.
"Ok, here's the price list, I shall see you chaps here 9am next Saturday."

Alfred and Eddie made their way up the stairs and out into daylight.
"I can't wait to record the time bandit through that Boeing console!" declared Eddie enthusiastically, "It's going to be awesome!"

"The path to success is to take massive, determined action" is a quote by motivational speaker Tony Robbins.

Chapter 7 - The Studio

"How much?" barked Alfred's dad as he looked at the studio price list.
"Frank the producer said that he can make even the most terrible band sound amazing." replied Alfred.
"Let's hope so," muttered his dad under his breath.
"Well I see how hard you've been working on this and how much it means to you."
He handed his son an envelope full of cash to pay for the recoding session and demo CD that he needed to enter the competition.
Saturday finally arrived after a week of mock exams and lunchtime rehearsals. The trio made their way across town to Hightown Studios. On arrival, Frank the producer made them feel at ease with a mug of steaming hot green tea.
They set up their instruments and sound checked the microphone levels.
"Testing 1, 2, 3," said Alfred with a warm glow in his cheeks as he took another gulp of tea."
The band played through three songs. Frank twiddled knobs and faders and brought out more tea and biscuits from the control room.
When Frank signalled that he was ready to record, the

band began to play and something extraordinary happened. All the nervous anticipation and self doubt that Alfred had endured up to this point suddenly subsided and was replaced by an inner feeling of calm and confidence. A hazy mixture of happiness and contentment came over him whilst gliding through the key changes of the songs. It appeared the other two felt the same way as Knuckles refrained from his normal excessive use of the crash cymbals and Eddie, who would normally be needlessly tweaking the controls on the time bandit was absorbed in the song. Both now appeared to focus wholeheartedly on the notes being played, resulting in a guitar track oozing with soul.

"Come through and have a listen guys,"
suggested Frank after they finished recording. Alfred, Eddie and Knuckles squeezed into the narrow cockpit and perched on seats behind Frank who was busy flicking overhead switches.

"Brace yourselves!" teased Frank as he pressed play on the blackbox recorder.

This was the first time the trio had heard themselves on a recording and the sound was epic. They listened through several times, gazing up at the glowing valves feeling like they were lost in a dream.

Several hours passed as Frank brought out more green tea whilst mixing the track onto CD. He played them some of his recent studio sessions which included a Gregorian Chant sung by Benedictine Monks, a man called Shane playing a didgeridoo and an EP featuring the charismatic vocals of local songwriter Tony Magpie.

"Blimey, we'd better get going!" said Alfred looking at his watch. He handed Frank the producer the envelope full of cash and collected a handful of CDs as they all made their way out into the evening rush hour.

"Thanks for the tea!" mumbled Eddie as he stumbled over the threshold.

"No problem, any time." replied Frank.

They made their way across town armed and ready with the music that might just be their ticket to the hottest gig in Hightown.

Frank the producer

Chapter 8 - The Radio Show

As soon as the school bell rang on Monday afternoon, Alfred ran out of the building and made his way to the Apollo Theatre.

"I'd like to enter my band into the competition," he explained to the lady at the reception.

"Fill out this form and Alan Van Dyke will announce the contestants on his Monday night radio show." replied the helpful lady.

Alfred filled out the form and handed over the CD.

"If you've been successful you'll be required to play here on Saturday the 17th" she added.

Alfred made the long journey back home, full of hope and anticipation for the week ahead. Unfortunately, the cold light of day was less exciting as the following week involved revision, exams and more revision for Alfred as he stared gloomily at his town planning Geography course work.

"You need to get good grades if you want to go to University," stated Alfred's mum as she stirred the cauliflower cheese sauce. But there was only really one question on Alfred's mind; would Alan Van Dyke play the Time Bandits on his drive time radio show?

The hype and anticipation was palpable in Alfred's house that Monday evening. Eddie and Knuckles had come over and they all sat around the kitchen table staring at the little Roberts radio waiting for the result, which for these young musicians felt like a World Cup final penalty shoot out.

Finally the song by The Lighthouse Family came to an end and Mr. Van Dyke addressed the nation.

"The first unsigned band to make it through to the competition are..."

He paused for effect and added suspense...

"The Tony Magpie band!"

"Who?" asked Alfred's dad with a dumbfounded expression on his face.

"They're a gospel rock band." replied Alfred, trying hard to conceal his disappointment.

"The second band to go through are..." said the DJ adding another dramatic pause,

"Artichoke Wind!"

"Oh for heavens sake!" cried Eddie, throwing his arms up in disbelief.

"The third act to make it through to the competition are...The Cynical Brothers!"

declared Mr. Van Dyke enthusiastically, who was now clearly enjoying his role as grandmaster, keeping the audience on tenterhooks.

"The fourth band to make it the the competition are…The Creepers!"
"You are having a giraffe!" shouted Knuckles, who up until this point had remained uncharacteristically silent but was now cracking his knuckle joints in disapproval at the nomination of this local pop rock band.
"The final unsigned band to go through to play to a panel of judges this Saturday at the Apollo Theatre and to be in with a chance of playing at the one and only Hightown Festival is…" rambled Mr. Van Dyke with added drama and an extra long pause,
"The Time Bandits!"
The kitchen erupted with joy and relief as Alfred, Eddie and Knuckles punched the air in defiance whilst Alfred's dad pulled his weary head out of his hands and was now reduced to an emotional wreck by the ordeal.
The DJ then proceeded to play a song by each of the five selected bands and Alfred realised that in order to win the competition they were going to have to pull an enormous rabbit out of the hat. However, in this moment he was filled with joy and relief considering what he and his band mates had achieved which only six weeks ago was merely a dream. They had made it to The Battle of the Bands!

The days leading up to the competition had not been quite as successful and not without setbacks. At their final lunch break rehearsal the pale shadowy figure of Neil Artichoke entered into the room, his hair slick with gel and sporting a deadpan expression on his face.

"Congratulations on making it to the competition, it's amazing that you got this far." said Neil through gritted teeth.

"What's that?" the prefect was now pointing at Eddie's unfinished guitar and looking aghast.

"It's a guitar time machine." replied Eddie

"Well it certainly looks like something from the Dark Ages!" Neil looked disapprovingly at the instrument. "It will do you good to know that the judges will be looking for a band with stage presence, charisma and the ability to control an audience." he paused before continuing, "You should at least cut your hair!"

This remark was the final straw for Knuckles,

"Who do you think you are Artichoke, my uncle?"

"I do not wish to ruffle any feathers, I am merely pointing out that perhaps you should change your name to The Tramps!"

Neil smirked and made a swift exit. At this point, the red faced Knuckles was clambering over his drum kit like a spaniel trying to get to a rat, sending drumsticks

high into the air and cymbals crashing all around, before finally ending up in a heap on the floor and dislocating his shoulder in the process.
Their final rehearsal before the competition was over.

"Where focus goes, energy flows" is a quote by motivational speaker Tony Robbins.

Chapter 9 - The day of reckoning

Morale in the Time Bandit camp was low as the trio waited anxiously backstage. Seeds of doubt had been sown in Eddie's mind about the aesthetics of his beloved guitar and Knuckles who had his arm in a sling had been in a foul mood ever since sustaining the shoulder injury.

The judges took to their seats at the front of the Theatre and introduced themselves to the audience:

Alfred looked at the running order and saw that his band were fourth in the line up to perform:

1) The Cynical Brothers
2) The Tony Magpie band
3) Artichoke Wind
4) The Time Bandits
5) Creepers

The first band who appeared on stage were a dance rock band with long hair and big guitar solos. Anna Kapranna of the Hightown Echo was scribbling frantically in her notebook during their performance whilst Jonny Agro, the retired bass player of The Sticky Things was swaying to the beat, clearly enjoying himself.
The second band arrived on stage in a haze of fog and once the smoke cleared, the crowd could just about make out the tall figure of Tony Magpie who was wearing a long white robe. His music was dark and heavy and his band seemed to have a dedicated army of followers at the front of the stage. Bob Sandy, Hightown's mayor looked baffled by this performance but nevertheless watched on with intrigue.

Next to perform were the defending champions Artichoke Wind. The crowd went berserk as they tried to get a glimpse of the charismatic crooner that was Neil Artichoke. The front row went wild as he slid across the stage with ease like a slippery Shakin' Stevens (ask your gran)! The band gave a bow at the end of their second song and left the stage to rapturous applause and chants of "We love you Neil!" This was not helping Alfred and Eddie with their pre-gig nerves as it was now the turn of The Time Bandits to take to the stage. Knuckles had made a last minute dash to the loos and was nowhere to be seen. Eddie hastily plugged in the TB1 guitar and programmed it to the year 1900 whilst Alfred made a desperate search for his drummer.

"Where is he?" asked Eddie.

"I dunno." replied Alfred nervously.

In the nick of time Knuckles ran on stage and quickly counted them in to play their first song. They played it much faster than usual and by the time they got to the second song, sweat was trickling down Eddie's brow onto his fretboard making it even harder to play. Alfred tried and failed to signal to Knuckles to slow it down but it was no use. Knuckles was drumming like a runaway train 100% locked into the tempo with his eyes closed.

He started off 'Flight of the rockin' bumblebee' at 160 beats per minute leaving Eddie scrambling around the fretboard looking for the notes as he darted around the A minor chromatic scale like a madman!
Alfred had by now given up trying to get the attention of his drummer and had noticed smoke appearing from the back of Eddie's guitar. This was not good! It was now apparent to Alfred that Eddie was in fact ON FIRE!
'Flight of the rockin' bumblebee' was now about to reach a dizzy climax as smoke was now billowing out of Eddie's rear end!
At first it appeared to the audience that this could possibly be part of the performance until Alfred dropped his guitar and started whacking Eddie's bottom with a guitar case. Up until this point Eddie had also remained blissfully unaware until he heard his band mate shouting,
"You're on fire Eddie!"
Eddie could now see his velvet jacket was alight, moreover, his guitar was also making strange noises. Alfred went off stage to find a fire extinguisher as Eddie took off his guitar and jacket and looked on in horror. The stage manager came running on extinguishing the flames and covering Eddie's groaning guitar with foam.

The panel of judges looked bewildered by this performance. Anna Kapranna was scribbling in her notebook faster than ever, clearly readers of the Hightown Echo would enjoy reading about this particular show at the Apollo Theatre.
The Time Bandits performance was well and truly over.

Chapter 10 - Anything is possible

After the stage had been cleared, the forlorn trio made their way outside to get some air and lick their wounds.
"Well that's ten months work gone up in smoke," muttered Eddie tearfully.
"Not to mention probably the best invention since the microwave." he added with a sniff.
"Sorry," murmured Knuckles, "I didn't mean to start the song that fast, but the lights were so bright and I couldn't hear anything." he added gloomily.
At that moment Tony Magpie appeared still in his white robes and gave Eddie a big hug.
"That was probably the best performance on stage since Jimi Hendrix!" declared Tony.
"Thanks," replied Eddie "Although Hendrix set his guitar alight on purpose!"
Tony paused to think before continuing,
"That's true, although you guys can really play. I've made more mistakes and had more setbacks in my life than you can possibly imagine."
Tony lowered his sunglasses to reveal dark bags beneath his piercing blue eyes before adding,

"Setbacks are required, mistakes are required…it's the only way to improve. If you can overcome the pain and fear that come with setbacks, anything is possible."

He then pushed his sunglasses back up his nose and disappeared into the theatre with his white robes flowing behind him. Alfred, Eddie and Knuckles had been outside for so long that they completely missed the fifth and final act by The Creepers.

They made their way back into the Theatre just as the judges were deliberating amongst themselves as to whom they would declare the winner of the competition. The mayor of Hightown, Bob Sandy finally got to his feet and took the microphone to make the announcement.

"A big thank you to the Apollo Theatre for once again holding this event, and an even bigger thank you to the catering department who have put on an a delightful spread of tea and cakes for the judges."

Alan Van Dyke was now devouring his fourth iced doughnut and was nodding his head in approval. The mayor took another belgian bun and a large swig of tea before continuing,

"The depth of talent we have seen today in Hightown is staggering…but there can only be one winner."

He took another slurp of his tea.

"And the winner is….. Artichoke Wind!"

Eddie rolled his eyes in disbelief as Neil Artichoke ran onto the stage to address his fans and collect his award.

"We are soooooo chuffed to win the competition for the fourth year in a row." boasted Neil.

He then proceeded to thank his entire family before reciting to the audience his family motto.

"An Artichoke never quits!"

The band came on stage and played their winning song one more time, much to the delight of the front row who appeared to be hardcore Artichoke fans.

Alfred, Eddie and Knuckles collected their instruments (what was left of them), and met up with their mums and dads who had been watching the chaos unfold from the upper balcony. They did their best to offer encouragement but the trio found it hard to conceal their disappointment.

They said their goodbyes and went their separate ways. Alfred found himself awake until the early hours of the morning, pondering the wise words of Tony Magpie, desperately clinging onto anything vaguely positive to help him overcome his limiting beliefs. He repeated to himself,

"If you can overcome the pain and fear of setbacks, anything is possible."

The following morning after his mum and dad came back from Hightown's largest car boot sale (as they did every Sunday morning, with the Renault 4 rammed full of antiques and other vintage items) Alfred's dad had a surprise for him.
"This is for you."
Alfred looked confused as his dad placed an envelope in his hands. He gingerly opened it to reveal two day tickets to the Hightown Festival.
"Jumping butterballs!" Alfred exclaimed excitedly.
"You may not be able to play there, but you can still go and enjoy yourself." his dad smiled as he added,
"It might cheer Eddie up too!"
Tears of joy started to well up around Alfred's eyeballs as he hugged his mum and dad and realised he would get to see the greatest rock band on the planet after all!

"AN ARTICHOKE NEVER QUITS"

Chapter 11 - The Hightown Festival

The sun had got its hat on for the festival weekend as Alfred and Eddie got off the bus and arrived at the site. They were met with the many sights and sounds that festivals have to offer including the intoxicating smell of burgers and diesel. They had arrived!
They made their way to the main stage where their music teacher Mr. Harmonic and his Rhythm and Blues band were playing (as they did every year) to an enthusiastic crowd. As the revellers were basking in the glorious sunshine, Alfred and Eddie were joined by Frank the producer who was wearing camouflage trousers and sipping hot green tea from a thermos flask.
"I took it upon myself to remix one of your tracks," Frank continued, "Do you guys like Mr. Scary?"
Alfred had an incredulous expression on his face,
"Like them?...We love 'em!"
He smirked, "You're going to love what I've done then!"
Frank said convincingly whilst taking another gulp of tea from his flask."
"Come over to the studio next Saturday and have a listen," offered Frank.

"Sounds great, thanks Frank!" replied Alfred as they wondered off in search of refreshments.

After stocking up on hotdogs and chips, Alfred and Eddie went for a ride on the helterskelter (a decision they would later regret) before making their way back to the stage to watch Artichoke Wind begin their fourth performance at the event.

"It could be you guys playing there next year," said a voice from behind them. Mr. Harmonic had appeared fresh off the stage to watch his students perform.

"Hi Mr. Harmonic, we really enjoyed listening to your band," enthused Alfred as the band were beginning to take to the stage.

"Thanks lads, we're not at school now though, call me Phil."

Their teacher continued, "You need to build up your skills, build them up until you become unstoppable! And you've got to rebuild that incredible guitar, I have honestly never heard anything quite like it!"

At that moment, Neil Artichoke and his band appeared on stage, however out of the corner of his eye Alfred couldn't help but notice a familiar looking man standing by the speakers with long black hair and cowboy boots.

"It can't be" thought Alfred to himself, straining his eyes to get a better view.

"Blimey Eddie, look who it is!"
The Mr Scary guitarist Kevin Slaughter was stood over by the sound desk talking to a couple of fans who had recognised him. Alfred and Eddie made their way over to him.
"Excuse me Kevin?"
Alfred asked, trying not to get starstruck whilst Eddie frantically searched in his coat for a pen.
"Would it be ok to get an autograph?"
"Sure, no problem," replied Kevin.
He took Eddie's felt tip pen and signed both his and Alfred's t-shirts before saying,
"Are you guys looking forward to the gig later?
"Oooooh yes!" exclaimed Alfred excitedly
"We'll be down the front!" added Eddie.
Kevin Slaughter smiled, turned and was ushered away by his security guard as more people were beginning to gather to catch a glimpse of the rock star.

Later that evening, as the sun was beginning to set on the village of Hightown, Alfred and Eddie made their way to the front of the crowd that had gathered to see the headline act. Alfred thought of all the wonderful people he'd met over the last 67 days. He may not have got to play at the festival this year, but he had made some truly great friends and memories to last a lifetime. He had even got an autograph from his guitar hero! The lights dimmed on the stage and out of the darkness a huge water canon appeared. The crowd went wild as Mr Scary took to the stage. Within seconds, Alfred and Eddie were soaked from head to toe and about to experience the greatest rock show of their lives!

THE END

Readers of this book can find out more about Alfred and his musical adventures online at:

www.alfredthemusician.com

Printed in Great Britain
by Amazon

64005717R00007